For my brother
Britta Teckentrup

First North American edition published in 2013 by Boxer Books Limited.
First published in Great Britain in 2013 by Boxer Books Limited.
www.boxerbooks.com

Text and illustrations copyright © 2013 Britta Teckentrup
The right of Britta Teckentrup to be identified as the author and illustrator of this work
has been asserted by her in accordance with the Copyright, Designs and Patents Act, 1988.

ISBN 978-1-907967-53-5

1 3 5 7 9 10 8 6 4 2

Printed in China

The art for Clumsy Duck was prepared by hand-printing paper
which was scanned and manipulated into a digital form.

All of our papers are sourced from managed forests and renewable resources.

Clumsy Duck

Britta Teckentrup

Boxer Books

Clumsy Duck was very clumsy.
She had just fallen over . . . again!
Not a day went by without her
stumbling, tripping, or falling.
It was very frustrating!

"Hi there!" said Chick.

"Did you fall down?"

"Yes," said Clumsy Duck, "I did.

Why do I have to be so clumsy?"

"Don't worry," said Chick.

"Let's go for a walk together."

Duck and Chick went up the hill – twice!
The first time, Clumsy Duck tripped over a stone.

The second time, Clumsy Duck bumped into a tree.

Finally they reached the top of the hill.
"What a wonderful view," said Clumsy Duck.

They set off along the muddy path.
Then, with a *slip, squidge, splat,*
Clumsy Duck splashed down in the mud!

"Oh, quack!" said Clumsy Duck.
Chick couldn't help a little chuckle.
"Come on," he said gently.
"Let's go to the pond and get you cleaned up!"

Clumsy Duck was worried.

Were her feet really that enormous?

Was there anything she could do?

Clumsy Duck and Chick waddled
and hopped along, not saying a word.

"Wow!" said Chick. "Look at your footprints. They're enormous! No wonder you are falling over all the time."

When they reached the pond,
Clumsy Duck asked,
"Why are my feet so big?"

"I don't know," answered Chick,
"but I'm sure there's a good reason.
Let's try and find out."

"Hmmm," mumbled Chick,
"maybe you can run really fast.
Come on, catch me."
Clumsy Duck chased after him.

She could waddle a lot faster
than she thought.
Until—*flump*!
"Never mind," said Chick.
"Let's try something else."

"Your big feet might be good for perching on a branch," said Chick.
Chick showed Duck how it was done.
Clumsy Duck jumped up too.
But her feet couldn't get a grip.
Poor Clumsy Duck fell off.
"Never mind," said Chick.
"Let's try something else."

"Maybe your feet are good for hopping?"
said Chick. Chick was good at hopping and
hopped onto a large flat stone next to the
pond.
"Copy me, Duck!"

But Clumsy Duck was not good at hopping!
She tripped, slipped, and then splashed
into the pond.

Chick stared at Clumsy Duck in amazement.
"Look at you!" squealed Chick.
"You're the fastest, bestest, most elegant
swimmer I've ever seen."

And it was true.

Clumsy Duck was not clumsy in the pond.

She moved across the water like a ballerina.

"That's it, Duck!" cried Chick.
"Your feet are perfect for swimming!
If I could swim like you, I wouldn't mind
being clumsy on land!"
Duck was happily gliding around the pond.

And from that day on, Duck didn't mind one little bit that she was a clumsy duck on land because she was such a wonderful swimmer in the water!